I WONDER IF
HERBIE'S HOME YET

I WONDER IF HERBIE'S HOME YET

WORDS BY MILDRED KANTROWITZ

PICTURES BY TONY DE LUNA

SMOKEY

HERBIE

LESTER

PARENTS' MAGAZINE PRESS/NEW YORK

for Susan and Amy

Hello...Mr. Franklin?
This is Smokey.
Is Herbie home?
He went skating...with Lester?
LESTER PINKNEY?
No, no message. 'bye.

Boy, that Herbie is one big fink!
That's a real friend.
A real NO-GOOD friend—
that's what Herbie is.
I mean what good is Saturday
if your best friend's not around?
Lester Pinkney...
Lester Pinkney just happens to be
the clumsiest kid on the block.
Lester Pinkney just happens to be
the smartest kid in the class.
I just don't happen to like
Lester Pinkney.

It couldn't be because of what happened
after school yesterday.
Couldn't be.
I mean I only said, "Herbie—
you're asking to borrow
the only thing I ever wanted
in my whole life.
My birthday present.
It's not even scratched up yet.
Ask me for anything else.
Ask me for anything else but my
new, red, high-rise banana bike."

He didn't ask me.
He just looked as I ran my hands
over those neat silver handle bars.
Then he said, "So long, Smokey,"
and walked away.
He didn't seem to be mad.
We didn't have a fight or anything
like that.
All he said was, "So long, Smokey."
It's like saying, "See you tomorrow."
Only you don't have to SAY it. That is,
if you're really good friends.

I'd give him anything else.
Anything else but my new
red banana bike.
Just last Saturday, we were sitting around,
doing nothing special,
and I asked him what we should do—
and Herbie said, "Eat."
And I said, "Like what?"
And he said, "Something sweet and cold."

So I got the dollar I had been saving
and we went down to CHARLIE'S.
We sat on the stools and ordered the
biggest, gooiest, ice-cream sundaes
you ever saw.
Then Herbie said, "O.K. if I pay you tomorrow?"
And I said, "My treat."
"You, Smokey Silver," he said, shaking my hand,
"are a great friend."
Then I said, "It's nothing. Forget it."
Well, he sure did!

Then how about the time
he was going away with his family
for the weekend.
There was Herbie, standing outside
my front door that Friday night.
Herbie, with the gerbil, the dog, the food,
the cage, the bed.
He didn't have to ask. I knew.
So I said, "Sure, I'll take care of them
for you. What's a best friend for?"
I remember saying, "Herbie, you forgot
to bring over the top to the cage."

I remember Herbie saying, "He'll never
make it over the top. He can't climb."
Well, he could. And he did.
Would you believe I spent
most of that Saturday tracking down
the gerbil?

And that dumb dog!
That dumb, homesick dog
kept barking and shivering—from
loneliness, I guess. I had to sleep
in the basement with him to keep him quiet.
When Herbie came home, he said, "I can
never repay you."
And I said, "It was nothing. Forget it."
And he sure must have!

I'll show him.
I'll take all my old comic books
and set up my own stand and
sell them all by myself and I'll
take the money and buy some new
comic books—and maybe some potato chips
and soda.
I'll get all the kids over and we'll
have a party right here
on my front stoop
where Herbie can see us and
will HE be sorry!

Maybe there's a ball game
down at the park.
Maybe I'll "ump."
Maybe I'll catch.
Maybe I'll hit a home run.
Maybe Herbie will see me.
Herbie usually plays shortstop.
I never told him, but you know —
he's a pretty rotten shortstop.
I never told him, 'cause you don't
to your best friend. But now...

BUTTERFINGERS! Do you hear me, Herbie? BUTTERFINGERS!

"Hello, Smokey. Home from the dentist so soon?"

I look up. Herbie's mother!

"Dentist," I say. "What dentist?"

"Why, Herbie said you had a dental appointment
this morning."

Holy cow!

I leave her standing there.

I take off and I'm running like

Niagara Falls right down to the bottom

of the hill.

Fifteen steps up.

RING THE BELL AND WALK IN.

So I do...right over to the lady

in white at the desk.

She knows I'm late.

I wish she wouldn't say it. She nods her head—
"You're late," she says, pointing to
the one empty seat.
"I forgot," I say. "Would you believe it?"
She nods her head and points to
the seat again.
She never says much. She just nods and points.
I sit and I wait and I
wonder if Herbie's home yet.

If I could call him, I'd say,
"Herbie, Lester Pinkney is ALL RIGHT!"
I'd say, "Herbie, you're a great shortstop."
I'd say, "You've got a great brain.
You never forget anything!"
I'd say, "Herbie, you can borrow my
bike, any time you like.
And for as long as you want it."
And he'd say, "You're great."
And I'd say, "It's nothing. Forget it."

I wonder if Herbie's home yet...

MILDRED KANTROWITZ is the author of *Maxie,* published by Parents' Magazine Press and selected as one of the best books of the year 1970 by the *School Library Journal.* Mrs. Kantrowitz studied painting and sculpture at Pratt Institute, the Art Students League, the Brooklyn Museum School and the New School. She has worked as an interior display designer and an assistant art director in publishing. Born in Brooklyn, she now lives in the historic Brooklyn Heights district with her husband and two daughters, Amy and Susan.

TONY DE LUNA has illustrated many picture books for young readers including *The Twelve Days of Christmas, Whose Little Red Jacket?* and *I Want to Be Little.* A native New Yorker, Mr. De Luna graduated from the College of the City of New York and studied art at Cooper Union. A collector as well as an artist, he owns over 500 old and rare books for children, plus some 2,500 comic books. He lives in Brooklyn with his collection and his wife and three children.